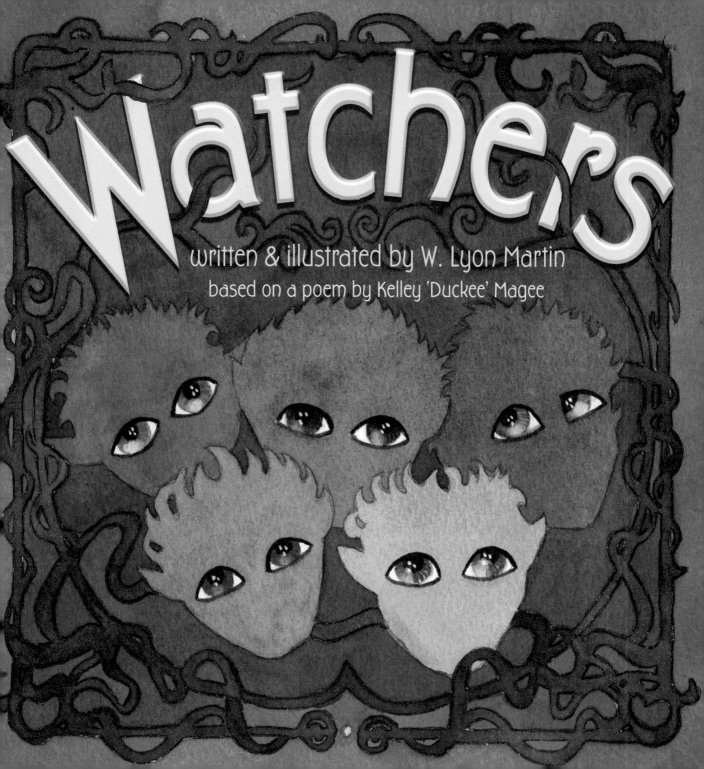

Watchers

written & illustrated by W. Lyon Martin

based on a poem by Kelley 'Duckee' Magee

They hide all over my room at night,
Waiting 'til Mama turns out my light.
I know they sneak closer, coming near,
Secret voices whisper in my ear.

At night they surround
me when I sleep.
So I plan to catch them
where they creep.
I'm always falling
asleep too fast,
But tonight I'll stay
awake at last.

I'm making a trap, now it's all set
I'm using a large bag not a net.
I'll catch who's sneaking around my room.
I'll stop being afraid very soon.

I strain to keep my eyes from closing,
I lie still, pretending I'm dozing.
Now I will catch one you wait and see,
I will catch who is frightening me.

I hear their whispers coming closer.
They are monsters or something grosser.
My body's shaking as if I'm cold.
But I act braver I'm being bold!

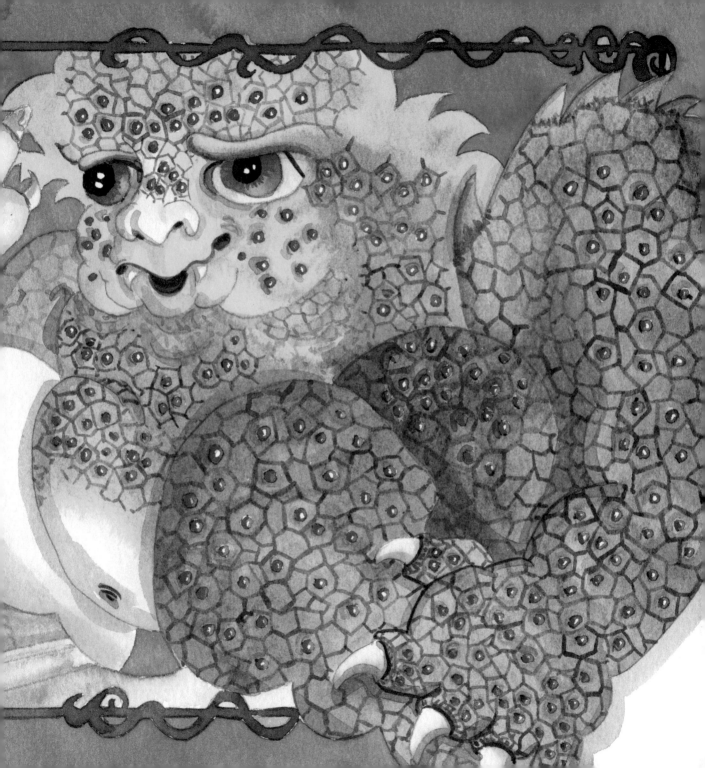

I refuse to lose myself in dreams,
They're creeping closer, or so it seems
I count all their eyes within the gloom,
Five pairs are watching around my room.

My trap is sprung, and something wiggles,
My great bag holds them. I hear giggles.
They fight to be free, jumping, jabbing.
My hand slides in, ready for grabbing.

I've finally I caught 'em, look and see,
I am holding them in front of me!

I expect a creature, great in size,
But what I find is a big surprise!

Five little fairies
around my bed,

One at my feet.

One at my head.

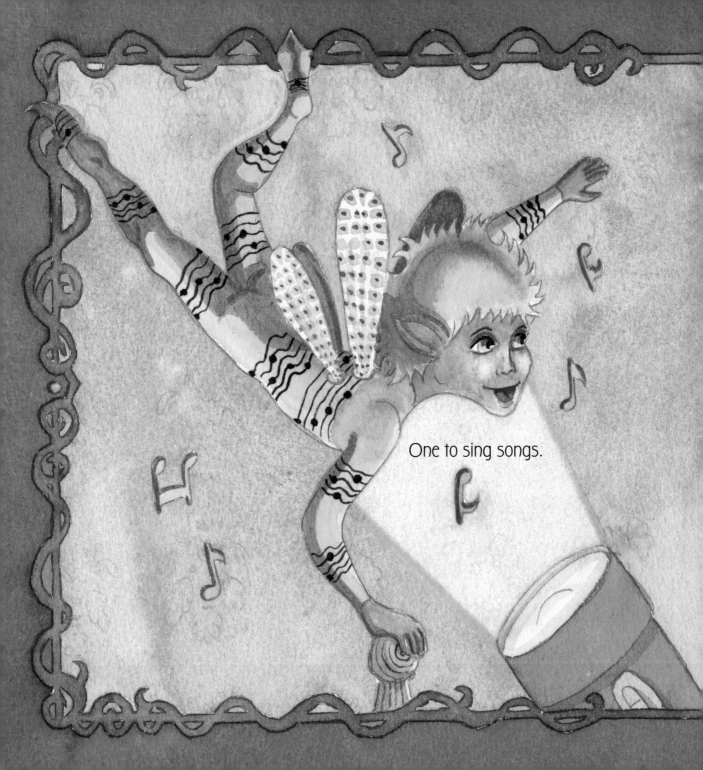

One to sing songs.

And one more to play.

And one to chase
scary dreams away.

Now I can fall asleep with a smile.
My friends will shoo away anything vile.
Five little fairies guard me all night,
Tiptoeing softly off at first light.

Magical Child Books
an imprint of Shades of White
Crystal City, MO
www.paganchildrensbookpublishing.info

Watchers

The illustrations were created in watercolor, gouache and pencil on 140lb Kilimanjaro cold press. Text was set in Hardwood LP.

ISBN-13 978-0-9796834-5-9

Publisher's Cataloging-in-Publication Data
Martin, W. Lyon.
    Watchers / written and illustrated by W. Lyon Martin.
    p. cm.
    "Based on a poem by Kelley 'Duckee' Magee"
    ISBN 9780979683459
    Summary: Who's hiding in corners and watching in the dark? A trap is set and our hero receives a big surprise when the watchers are finally captured.
[1. Fairies--Fiction. 2. Bedtime--Fiction. 3. Stories in rhyme.] II. Title.

PZ7.L9883 WAT 2008
[E]--dc22   2007904405

Printed on recycled paper in the United States by Corporate Graphics Commercial, North Mankato, MN 56003

Acknowledgements

I met Kelley in 2006, shortly after my first book was published, while I was making one of my first appearances as a new author/illustrator.

She was pregnant with her now 2-year-old twin boys. During the weekend event, we became fast friends and she confided in me how she wished she had the talent to take her grandmother's gift and create a children's book from it.

In her own words below is the story she shared with me and the poem in its original form.

"When I was a little girl, my family moved from America to Germany. I got very homesick and I missed my grandparents a lot. Once, my Granny and GrandPa came all the way to Germany to visit. I told Granny how much I missed her. She told me she would leave me a present, and she taught me this bedtime prayer.

Five little fairies around my bed,
One at the foot, one at the head.
One to sing songs and one to play,
And one to take scary dreams away.

I grew up and had children of my own. When my daughter was too little to say prayers I made my Granny's present into a lullaby which I sang to her every night. My Granny died before my sons could meet her. I sing them 5 Little Fairies every night so they can still get to know at least a little bit about her. I know she is in Heaven with the fairies, or maybe she is one of the 5 little fairies now, watching over my children."

I want to thank Kelley and her children for the wonderful opportunity to share their family memory with you. I also want to thank my family for putting up with my artistic angst while I made them listen 'only' one more time to the story as I got it 'just right." I love you all.

MAGICAL BOOKS FOR MAGICAL KIDS
Stories from Magical Child Books

An Ordinary Girl, A Magical Child
Take a joyful romp with Rabbit around the wheel of the Year as she learns about herself and her Pagan Ways in the first fully illustrated Pagan children's book to explore Wiccan magic, customs and holidays through a child's point of view.
ISBN-13 978-0-9796834-3-5
$16.95 Hardcover

Aidan's First Full Moon Circle
An enchanting, fictional tale of a Wiccan nighttime gathering will engage young readers with magical images while introducing some coven ritual basics.
ISBN-13 978-0-9796834-4-2
$16.95 Hardcover

Watchers
Who's hiding in corners and watching in the dark? A trap is set and our hero receives a big surprise when the watchers are finally captured. Young readers will request this bouncy bedtime tale even after they know the mystery.
ISBN-13 978-0-9796834-5-9
$16.95 Hardcover

Buy them at your local book store or use this convenient coupon for ordering.
Shades of White • 301 Tenth Avenue • Crystal City, MO 63019
Please send me the Magical Child Books I have checked, for which I am enclosing $ _____ (Please add $5.00 to cover postage and handling) Send Check or Money Order (no cash or C.O.D.s) or charge by MasterCard or Visa. Prices and numbers are subject to change without notice.
___ An Ordinary Girl, A Magical Child   ___ Aidan's First Full Moon Circle   ___ Watchers

Card#:_____ Exp Date: _____ Phone: _____

Name: _____ Address: _____

City: _____ State: _____ Zip: _____
For faster ordering by credit card call **314-740-0361** or visit us online at **www.paganchildrensbookpublishing.info**